To ....**LOLA**.........................

For being good.

Merry Christmas!

From **Santa**

Santa is coming to New York

Written by Steve Smallman
Illustrated by Robert Dunn

Copyright © Hometown World Ltd. 2019

Published by Sourcebooks Jabberwocky,
an imprint of Sourcebooks, Inc.
P.O. Box 4410, Naperville, Illinois 60567-4410
(630) 961-3900
jabberwockykids.com

Date of Production: May 2019
Run Number: 5014816
Printed and bound in China (1010)
10 9 8 7 6 5 4 3 2 1

Santa is coming to New York

Written by Steve Smallman
Illustrated by Robert Dunn

sourcebooks
jabberwocky

"Well?"

boomed Santa. "Have all the children from New York been good this year?"

"Well...uh...mostly," answered the little old elf, as he bustled across the busy workshop to Santa's desk.

Santa peered down at the elf from behind the tall, teetering piles of letters that the children of New York had sent him.

"Mostly?" asked Santa, looking over the top of his glasses.

"Yes...but they've all been especially good in the last few days!" said the elf.

"Jolly good!" chuckled Santa.
"Then we'd better get their presents loaded up!"

Even though the sack of presents was

really, really big
really, really

and the elves were ... small,

they seemed to have no trouble loading it onto Santa's sleigh.
Though how they managed to fit such a big sack onto one little sleigh
even they didn't know. But somehow they did.

"Splendid!" boomed Santa. "We're ready to go!"

"Er...not quite, Santa," said the little old elf. "One of our reindeer is missing!"

"Missing?

Which reindeer is missing?" asked Santa.

"The youngest one, Santa," said the elf. "It's his first flight tonight. I've called him and called him, but..."

Just then, a young reindeer strolled up, munching on a large carrot.

"Where have you been?"

asked Santa.

But the youngest reindeer was crunching so loudly that it was no wonder he hadn't heard the little old elf calling.

"Oh well, never mind," said Santa, giving the reindeer a little wink. He took out his Santa-nav and tapped in the coordinates for New York.

"This will guide us to New York in no time."

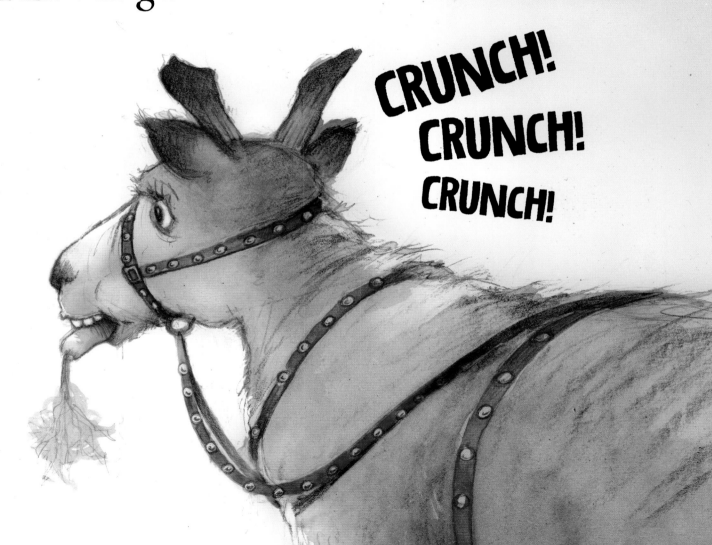

With a flick of the reins and a jerk of the harness, off they went, racing through the sky.

"Ho, ho, ho!"

laughed Santa.

"We'll soon have these presents delivered to the Empire State!"

Santa's sleigh flew through the starry night heading south across the Arctic Ocean. On they flew in the wintry air over Canada. In the wink of an eye, the sleigh was flying above Vermont, and on over Albany on the left. The youngest reindeer was very excited. He had never been away from the North Pole before.

They had just crossed the East River
when, suddenly, they ran into a blizzard.
Snowflakes whirled around the sleigh.

They couldn't see a thing!

The youngest reindeer was getting a bit worried,
but Santa didn't seem concerned.

"In two miles..."

said the Santa-nav in a bossy lady's voice,

"...keep left at the next star."

"But, ma'am," Santa blustered, "I can't see any stars in all this snow!"
Soon they were

hopelessly lost!

Ding-dong!
Ding-dong!

Then, through the
howling blizzard, the
youngest reindeer heard
a faint, ringing sound.

Ding-dong!

He looked over at the old reindeer
with the red nose. But he had
his head down.

(Red nose...I wonder
who that could be?)

Ding-dong!
Ding-dong!

Ding-dong! Ding-dong!

There was that sound again,
like church bells ringing.
The youngest reindeer turned
around to look at Santa.
But Santa wasn't listening.
He seemed to be arguing
with a little box with
buttons on it.

With a flick of the
harness and a jerk of the
reins, the youngest reindeer gave
a sharp **TUG** and headed off toward
the sound of the bells, pulling Santa
and his sleigh behind him!

"Whoa!"

cried Santa, pulling his hat straight. "What's going on?" Then, to his surprise, he heard the ringing sound.

"Well done, young reindeer!" he shouted cheerfully. "It must be the bells of St. Patrick's Cathedral. Don't worry, children, Santa is coming!"

Then, suddenly...

CRUNCH!

The sleigh hit something as it
plummeted through the snow clouds.
"You have arrived!"
said the Santa-nav unhelpfully.

Finally, when the snow had died down and the clouds parted, Santa discovered exactly where they were...

...stuck, right at the very top of the
Empire State Building!

"Everybody, PULL!"

The reindeer **PULLED** with all their might until, at last,
with a screeching noise, the sleigh scraped clear of the
Empire State Building and Santa steered them safely along
Fifth Avenue, past Rockefeller Center, St. Patrick's Cathedral,
and the Museum of Modern Art, over the Pond and the zoo,
into Central Park not far from the Alice in Wonderland statue.

Luckily, there
was no real
damage done, but
the packages had all
been jumbled up. Santa
quickly sorted out the
presents into order again.

"All right," said Santa. "Thanks
to this young reindeer I know where
we are now. Don't worry, children,

Santa is coming!"

Santa drove his sleigh expertly from rooftop to rooftop all over New York, popping in and out of chimneys as fast as he could go.

(Which was pretty fast for a chubby fellow!)

There were big chimneys in Buffalo and small chimneys in the Adirondacks. He squeezed down thin chimneys in Syracuse and plummeted down fat chimneys in Rochester, and tricky chimneys in the Catskills.

The youngest reindeer was amazed at how quickly they went. Santa never seemed to get tired at all! And it looked like the children in New York were going to be very lucky this year! But the youngest reindeer was starting to feel a bit weary and quite hungry, too!

He piled them under the Christmas trees
and carefully filled up the stockings
with surprises.

In house after house, Santa delved
inside his sack for packages of
every shape and size.

Santa took a little bite out of each cookie,
a tiny sip of milk, wiped his beard,
and popped the carrots into his sack.

In house after house, the good children
of New York had left out a large plate
of cookies, a small glass of milk,
and a big, crunchy carrot.

From the Bronx to Staten Island, from Manhattan to Queens, from Brooklyn to Downtown and ALL the places in between, Santa and his sleigh visited every house in New York.

Santa delivered presents to Andrew, Alison,
Anna, Arabella, Archie, Ashley...the list
went on and on!...Zac, Zara, Zeb, Zoe, Zybil.

(Zybil? That must be a
spelling mistake, surely!)

Finally, Santa had delivered the last present on his long New York list.

"Great moons and stars!" sighed Santa. "It's past midnight and my sack seems as heavy as ever! I hope I haven't forgotten anyone."

Santa opened his sack to check...but it was full of juicy, crunchy carrots!

Santa divided the carrots among all the reindeer.
"Well done!" he said, patting the youngest reindeer gently on the nose.

But the youngest reindeer didn't hear him...he was too busy munching!

Then it was time to set off for home. Santa reset his Santa-nav once more
to the North Pole, and soon they were speeding over the Hudson River,
toward the George Washington Bridge through the crisp, starry night.